GALACTIC ADVENTURES

PRESS

Los Angeles • New York

"Use the Force" adapted by Megan Ilnitzki. Art by Stephane Roux and Pilot Studio.
"Escape from Jabba's Palace" adapted by Brooke Vitale. Art by Stephane Roux and Pilot Studio.
"The Ewoks Join the Fight" adapted by Brooke Vitale. Art by Stephane Roux and Pilot Studio.

For information address Disney • Lucasfilm Press, 1101 Flower Street, Glendale, California 91201.
ISBN 978-1-4847-4207-5
F383-2370-2-15194
Printed in China
First Edition, July 2015
1 3 5 7 9 10 8 6 4 2

USE THE FORCE

Adapted by Megan Ilnitzki

Art by Stephane Roux and Pilot Studio

Luke Skywalker was on a mission.

"You will go to the Dagobah system," his old Jedi Master, Obi-Wan Kenobi, had told him. "There you will learn from Yoda, the Jedi Master who instructed me."

Now, as Luke turned his X-wing fighter toward the planet, R2-D2 beeped at him.

"That's it. Dagobah," Luke told R2-D2. "No, I'm not going to change my mind about this."

Luke checked his radar. "I'm not picking up any cities or technology. Massive life-form readings, though. There's something alive down there. . . ."

Luke turned his X-wing toward the planet. As he entered Dagobah's foggy atmosphere, his ship suddenly lost power. "All the scopes are down," he told R2. "I can't see a thing!"

Luke tried to land the X-wing, but it was out of control. The fighter crashed into a giant swamp. After climbing out of the fighter jet, Luke and R2-D2 swam to shore.

Luke was setting up camp when he heard a strange voice behind him. It was a small green alien.

"I am wondering, why are you here?" the alien asked.

"I'm looking for a Jedi Master," Luke said.

The alien nodded. "You seek Yoda. Take you to him I will. But now we must eat. Come!"

Luke had no choice. That strange alien seemed to know Yoda! Grumbling, Luke followed the creature back to his home.

As they ate, Luke complained to the little alien. "I don't understand why we can't see Yoda now," he said. "How far away is Yoda? Will it take us long to get there?"

"Not far," the alien replied. "Yoda not far."

The creature told Luke to be patient, but Luke was restless. He was eager to meet the Jedi Master.

"I don't even know what I'm doing here," he said. "We're wasting our time!"

The alien turned away from Luke. "I cannot teach him," he said. "The boy has no patience."

Suddenly, Luke heard another voice. It was Obi-Wan! Luke realized that the strange creature must be Yoda.

Reluctantly, Yoda agreed to train Luke.

Day after day, Luke worked with the Jedi Master. He raced through the swamp with the creature on his back. He swung on vines and used the Force to lift objects with his mind.

"A Jedi's strength flows from the Force," Yoda explained. "But beware of the dark side. If once you start down the dark path, forever will it dominate your destiny."

Yoda knew Luke could truly understand the dark side of the force only by facing it. He took Luke to a cave deep in the swamp.

"That place is strong with the dark side of the Force," Yoda told Luke. "A domain of evil it is. In you must go."

"What's in there?" Luke asked.

"Only what you take with you," Yoda replied.

As Luke crept down the cave's slimy passageway, the looming figure of Darth Vader emerged from the shadows. Angry, Luke drew his lightsaber and attacked. The two fought until at last Luke defeated the Sith Lord.

Suddenly, Darth Vader disappeared. He had been a figment of Luke's imagination. It had been a test.

Outside the cave, Yoda sadly shook his head. If Luke did not learn to control his emotions, the dark side would take him.

Luke still had much to learn. He was using the Force to lift objects when R2-D2 beeped in alarm. The X-wing was slipping farther into the swamp.

Luke watched in despair. "Oh, no. We'll never get it out now," he said.

Yoda stamped his foot in disapproval. "So certain, are you? Always with you it cannot be done. Hear you nothing that I say?" He wanted Luke to use the Force to lift the X-wing.

Luke looked at the sinking jet. "Master, moving stones around is one thing. This is totally different."

"No," Yoda replied. "No different! Only different in your mind. You must unlearn what you have learned."

Luke nodded. "Okay," he said. "I'll give it a try."

"No. Try not," Yoda said. "Do . . . or do not. There is no try."

Luke concentrated, straining to use the Force to move the X-wing. The fighter shook but did not move.

"I can't," Luke said. "It's too big."

"Size matters not," Yoda replied. "Look at me. Judge me by my size, do you? And well you should not. For my ally is the Force. And a powerful ally it is."

Yoda closed his eyes and focused his energy.

Luke watched in amazement as the X-wing rose out of the swamp and landed gently on the shore.

"I don't believe it," Luke said.

"That is why you fail," Yoda replied. Shaking his head, the Jedi Master turned away.

After that, Luke trained even harder. He listened to Yoda and practiced constantly. And he tried to learn to remain calm.

"Through the Force, things you will see," Yoda said. "Other places. The future. The past. Old friends long gone."

But when Luke tried to clear his mind, he suddenly saw a horrifying image of the future. "Han! Leia!" he called.

In his vision, Luke saw his friends. They had been captured by Darth Vader and were being tortured! Yoda warned him about his vision. "Always in motion, the future," he explained.

Luke wanted to stay and learn from Yoda, but he could not risk his friends' lives. He had to save them!

Climbing into his X-wing, Luke turned to Yoda. "Master Yoda, I promise to return and finish what I've begun. You have my word."

"Strong is Vader," Yoda warned. "Mind what you have learned. Save you it can."

"I will," Luke replied.

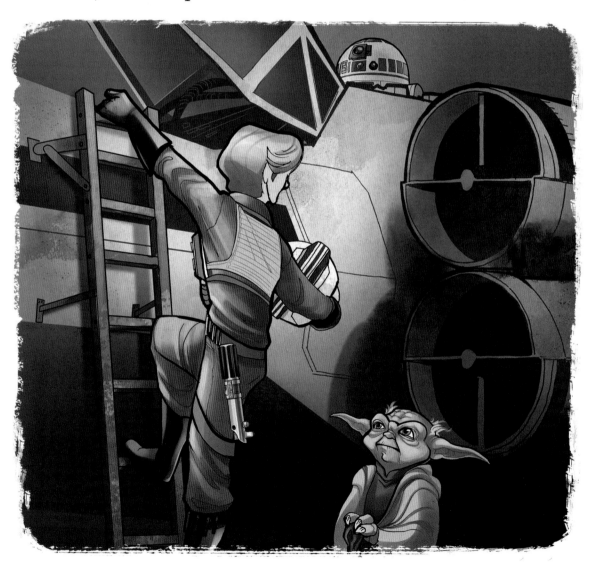

Luke fired up his X-wing, and then he and R2-D2 took off to find their friends.

Below them, Yoda shook his head sadly. "Reckless is he. Now, matters are worse."

Yoda knew that Vader planned to turn Luke to the dark side. He hoped the boy would be strong enough to resist.

As Luke flew through space, he thought about what he had learned from Yoda. He was ready to face Darth Vader and to use the Force to save his friends. But he would keep his promise to Yoda. He would return to Dagobah to complete his training as a Jedi.

ESCAPE FROM
JABBA'S PALACE

Adapted by Brooke Vitale

Art by Stephane Roux and Pilot Studio

Han Solo was in trouble. He had been captured by Darth Vader and frozen in carbonite. The Sith Lord had then given Solo to the bounty hunter Boba Fett.

Now the frozen hero was in the one place he had desperately been trying to avoid: the palace of Jabba the Hutt.

Han's friends knew they had to save him. But to do that, they would have to get inside the palace.

Luke Skywalker had a plan. He sent R2-D2 and C-3PO to Jabba with a hologram message.

"Greetings, Exalted One," Luke said. "I seek an audience with Your Greatness to bargain for Solo's life. As a token of my goodwill, I present to you a gift: these two droids."

Jabba looked at R2-D2 and C-3PO and laughed. "There will be no bargain," he said in Huttese. "I will not give up my favorite decoration."

Jabba was not about to give up the droids, either. C-3PO was assigned to work as a translator in the palace, and R2-D2 was sent to Jabba's sail barge.

Later that night, as Jabba celebrated his victory over Han, a loud noise shook the palace. Jabba's servants turned to see a bounty hunter enter the room. The bounty hunter had captured Chewie!

Jabba was thrilled. He and the bounty hunter agreed to a price, and Chewie was sent to the dungeon.

But this was no ordinary bounty hunter. It was Princess Leia in disguise!

That night, while everyone slept, she crept through Jabba's palace and freed Han.

Han's time in the carbonite had left him weak.

"I've got to get you out of here," Leia said.

As she helped Han to his feet, an evil laugh filled the room. It was Jabba! His servants took hold of the weakened Han and threw him in the dungeon with Chewie.

Back in the throne room, Jabba had taken Princess Leia prisoner. Suddenly, a mysterious visitor arrived. It was Luke.

Using his Jedi powers, he tried to trick Jabba into freeing his friends. "You will bring Captain Solo and the Wookiee to me," he said. "I warn you not to underestimate my powers."

"There will be no bargain, young Jedi," Jabba replied. "I shall enjoy watching you die."

Luke extended his hand and a blaster flew into it. He was using the Force! But he was not fast enough. The floor opened beneath him and he fell into a dark, musty pit.

Luke had fallen into the lair of the vicious rancor. All around him were the bones of the monster's victims.

Suddenly, a gate opened and the rancor stomped into the pit. The beast picked Luke up in one hand and opened its giant mouth.

But Luke was ready! He shoved a bone between the rancor's jaws so it couldn't bite down, and it dropped him.

Then, rushing past the beast, he threw a boulder at the gate's controls. The gate slammed down, crushing the rancor.

Jabba was not happy. He had expected his monster to defeat the Jedi!

At Jabba's order, Luke, Han, and Chewie were brought before him.

"Jabba the Hutt has decreed that you are to be terminated . . . immediately," C-3PO translated. "You will therefore be taken to the Dune Sea and cast into the Pit of Carkoon, the nesting place of the all-powerful Sarlacc."

Jabba watched from a large sail barge as his prisoners were transported on a skiff to the Pit of Carkoon. As they neared the pit, Luke turned to Jabba.

"This is your last chance," Luke yelled. "Free us or die!"

"Move him into position," Jabba replied.

On board Jabba's sail barge, R2-D2 quietly slipped away from the crowd. He watched from the window as Jabba's men pushed Luke toward the plank.

Luke stepped onto the plank over the Sarlacc pit. With a nod to R2-D2, he jumped!

Suddenly, R2-D2 shot an object into the sky. Luke grabbed the plank and sprang back onto the deck of the skiff.

Reaching out his hand, Luke took hold of the object. It was his lightsaber!

Luke wasted no time. He quickly freed Han and Chewie from their bonds, and the three jumped into battle with Jabba's guards. Enraged, Jabba ordered his men to open fire on the skiff.

Inside Jabba's barge, Princess Leia seized her moment to escape. Wrapping her chains around the evil gangster, she defeated him once and for all.

R2-D2 zapped Leia's chains and they broke apart.

"Come on," Leia said to R2-D2. "We've gotta get outta here."

While Luke fought off the rest of Jabba's men on the top deck of the sail barge, Leia aimed the ship's cannon at the deck. Holding on to each other, the friends swung to safety.

Reunited at last, the group soared across the desert of Tatooine. Behind them, Jabba's barge exploded.

They had defeated him. But more importantly, they had Han back. They were a team again.

THE EWOKS JOIN
THE FIGHT

Adapted by Brooke Vitale

Art by Stephane Roux and Pilot Studio

Luke Skywalker looked around the forest moon of Endor. He had landed there with Princess Leia, Han Solo, Chewbacca, R2-D2, and C-3PO. The rebels were on a mission. They were looking for a secret bunker that hid a special machine—a machine that could help them destroy the Death Star!

As the rebels snuck through the forest, they spotted two biker scouts.

"Should we try and go around?" Princess Leia asked.

"It'll take time," Luke replied.

But Han had an idea. "Chewie and I will take care of this," he said. "You stay here."

Luke warned Han to be quiet, but Han had other ideas. He snuck up on the stormtroopers and attacked!

As Han fought, more scouts appeared in the forest. Seeing the rebels, the scouts jumped on their speeder bikes and zoomed away.

Luke and Leia climbed aboard the first scouts' bikes and took off after the others. They couldn't let the stormtroopers warn the Empire of their presence on Endor.

"Keep on that one. I'll take these two," Luke called. And with that, he took off, leaving Leia behind.

Leia chased after the other scout. She managed to catch up to him, but then the scout fired his blaster at her. Leia tried to dodge the blast and fell off her speeder.

She was all alone in the forest, with no way to get back to her friends.

Suddenly, a small furry creature appeared. It was an Ewok. It poked at Leia with a sharp stick.

"Cut it out," Leia said, standing up and brushing herself off.

Leia sighed and walked over to a fallen tree. "Looks like I'm stuck here," she said, sitting down. "Trouble is, I don't know where here is!"

Leia looked at the Ewok again. "Maybe you can help me," she said.

Leia offered the Ewok some of her food, and he scrambled over, excited.

The Ewok was just getting comfortable with Leia when a blaster went off.

"Freeze!" a voice said. It was a stormtrooper!

Unseen by the scout, the Ewok crept into the bushes. Then, using a large stick, he hit the trooper. Together, Leia and the Ewok disarmed the scout.

"Come on. Let's get out of here," Leia said.

The Ewok nodded and took Leia's hand. Turning, he led her toward his village.

Meanwhile, Luke and his friends searched the forest for Leia. But all they found were two wrecked speeders and Princess Leia's helmet.

"I'm afraid that Artoo's sensors can find no trace of Princess Leia," C-3PO said.

Suddenly, Chewie noticed something. He reached out for what he thought was a tasty snack.

"Chewie, wait. Don't!" Luke called.

But he was too late. A giant net scooped up the friends and hoisted them high in the air.

As Han and Luke tried to get free, R2-D2 extended a saw. In no time, he had cut through the net.

Crash! The rebels fell to the ground. But they were no longer alone. A group of Ewoks surrounded them, and the furry creatures did not seem happy.

The Ewoks tied up the rebels and took them to their village. When they arrived, the rebels were surprised to see Princess Leia!

Leia tried to tell the Ewoks that Han and Luke were her friends, but they did not listen. Only C-3PO was allowed to remain free. The Ewoks seemed to think he was a powerful being.

"Threepio," Luke said. "Tell them if they don't do as you wish, you'll become angry and use your magic."

C-3PO tried to do as Luke said, but the Ewoks still wouldn't listen.

Closing his eyes, Luke used the Force to make C-3PO float.

The Ewoks were amazed. Now they *knew* the droid was powerful. They quickly did as he said and untied his friends.

That night, the Ewoks gathered around C-3PO, who told them tales of the rebels and Darth Vader.

The Ewoks liked the stories. And they liked the rebels.

They decided to make the rebels part of their tribe!

One of the Ewoks jumped up and began to hug Han. As he did so, he jabbered away. Han couldn't understand what the Ewok was saying.

"He says the scouts are going to show us the quickest way to the shield generator," C-3PO translated.

The next morning, the rebels and the Ewok scouts set out for the hidden bunker. Luke did not go along. He knew it was time to face Darth Vader.

"The main entrance to the control bunker is on the far side of that landing platform," Leia explained when they arrived. But the landing platform was surrounded by guards!

Luckily, the Ewoks knew of a back entrance. The rebels snuck around and surprised the Empire's scouts, quickly disarming them.

Han, Chewie, and Leia made their way deep inside the
bunker. But before they could turn off the Death Star's
shield generator, they were surrounded by Imperial soldiers.
It was a trap! The Empire had been waiting for them.

From their hiding places in the forest, the Ewoks
watched the Empire's scouts march Han, Leia, and Chewie
back out of the bunker. The Ewoks knew they had to do
something. With the help of C-3PO, they distracted the
scouts, drawing them away from Luke, Han, and Chewie.

The Ewoks knew just what to do.

They threw rocks at the stormtroopers. . . .

They destroyed the Empire's machines. . . .

They tripped the scouts and tied them up. . . .

With Chewie's help, the Ewoks took control of an All Terrain Scout Transport.

The group directed the vehicle to the bunker, where Han and Leia were in trouble. Han was about to fire at the AT-ST when the hatch popped open and Chewie appeared.

Just then, the doors to the bunker opened. The rest of the Empire's soldiers filed out, ready to defeat the rebels. But instead, they found themselves surrounded by Ewoks!

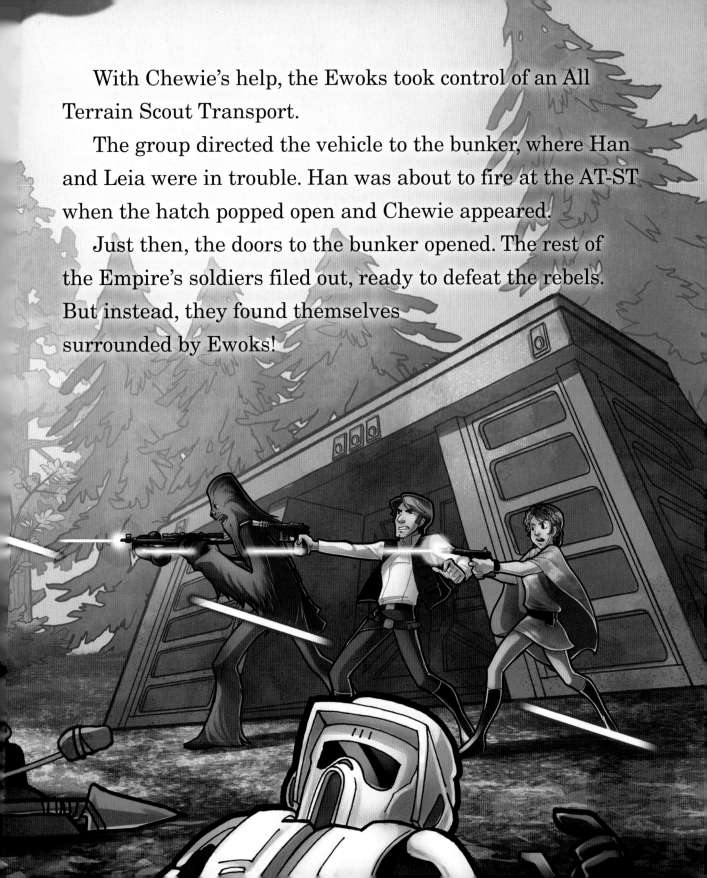

With the Imperial scouts taken care of, Han Solo did what he had gone to do. He blew up the bunker!

The shield generator was destroyed. The Death Star was vulnerable!

Thanks to the Ewoks, the rebels had a shot at beating the Empire. . . .